Floods and Blizzards

William B. Rice

Floods and Blizzards

Publishing Credits

Associate Editors
James Anderson
Torrey Maloof

Editorial Director
Dona Herweck Rice

Editor-in-Chief
Sharon Coan, M.S.Ed.

Creative Director
Lee Aucoin

Illustration Manager
Timothy J. Bradley

Publisher
Rachelle Cracchiolo, M.S.Ed.

Science Consultant
Scot Oschman, Ph.D.

Teacher Created Materials
5301 Oceanus Drive
Huntington Beach, CA 92649-1030
http://www.tcmpub.com

ISBN 978-1-4333-0313-5

Printed by : 465482
Printed In : Malaysia / PO#15080

Table of Contents

The Power of Water

Water can help a boat sail, but it can also flip the boat over. That is an old proverb, or saying. Like most proverbs, it is based in truth. Water is needed and useful, like when it helps a boat sail. It sustains life. It cleans. It can be used for both play and travel. Life cannot exist without it.

But water can also be terrible. Storms can flip and sink ships. Floods can wash away property and kill or strand people who are unable to reach higher ground. And water turned to snow can freeze, bury, and blind people in a whirling **blizzard** of white.

Mostly Water

About 70 percent of Earth is covered in water.

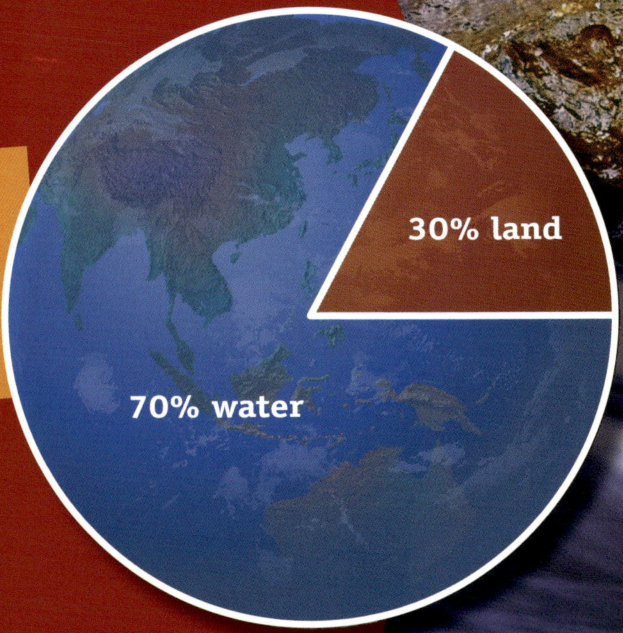

Streets become flooded quickly in Southeast Asia during the monsoon season.

Blizzards make it dangerous for people to travel away from their homes.

What Is a Flood?

A **flood** is a great overflow of water. It rushes over land that is usually not underwater. Floods can happen in an instant. There may be almost no warning that they are coming. People and property may be badly hurt by floods. Floods can change the land itself.

Heavy rains cause floods. Rainstorms may also create crashing waves, and those waves may cause floods. But it all starts with the rain.

Rain is part of the water cycle. The sun **evaporates** (i-VAP-uh-reyts) water from the Earth. The water turns to a gas and rises. It **condenses** (kuhn-DENS-es) in the air and becomes liquid again. It forms into small drops. The drops combine and become clouds. The clouds **precipitate** (pri-SIP-i-teyt). That means they release water as rain, snow, or hail. The water falls to the Earth and the cycle continues.

When a great deal of rain falls, the land and plants may not have the time or space to absorb it. Riverbeds and other water bodies may not be able to hold it. The extra water flows onto the land, and that is a flood.

Cloudy

The heaviest rain comes from **cumulonimbus** (kyoo-myuh-loh-NIM-buhs) clouds.

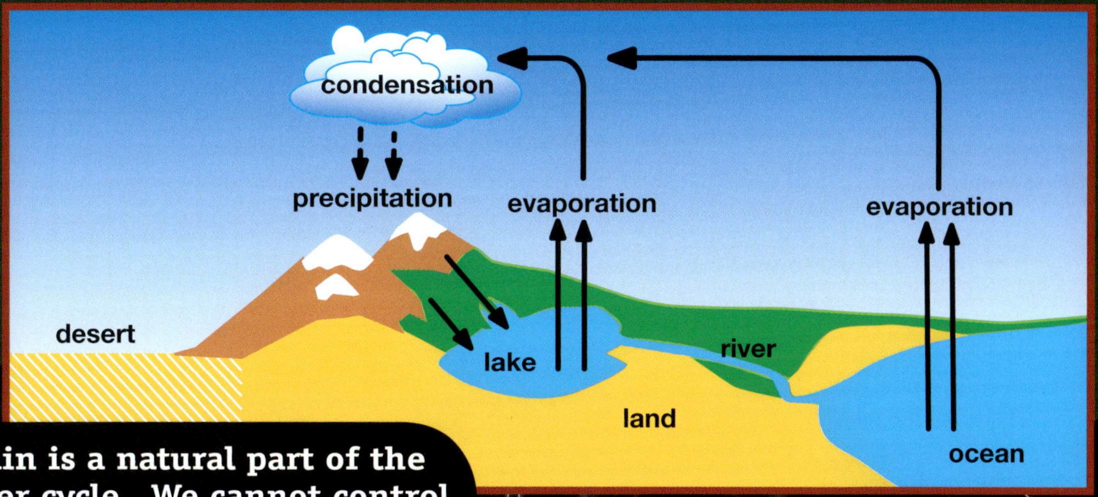

Rain is a natural part of the water cycle. We cannot control how much rain falls or stop floods from happening when there is too much rain.

Storms are the biggest cause of floods.

Big Rain

A lot of rain can fall in just a short amount of time. In 1975, more than 40 centimeters (16 inches) of rain fell in one hour in Beijing, China. In California in 1926, more than 2.5 centimeters (1 inch) of rain fell in just one minute!

A river in India overflows its floodplain banks as the result of a monsoon.

The most rain falls in places near and around the equator. The least rain falls in deserts. But floods can happen in both of these places. They can happen anywhere there is water.

River floods are a very common type of flood. They are caused most often by heavy rainfall. Melting snow can also flow into rivers and cause floods.

Rivers form over time in places where water normally flows. But when more water flows in than the river can hold, the water pours over the riverbanks. It covers the **floodplain**. The floodplain is the low land that runs alongside the river. Homes and businesses near the river are flooded as well. People may be stranded. Crops can be destroyed. People usually have some warning before these floods happen. It may take hours or days for the river to overflow.

Flash floods happen when a lot of rain falls in a small area in a short amount of time. They come in a flash, which is how they get their name. They are common in deserts. That is because the ground there is hard and dry. Water may not be able to soak in easily. It may come rushing across the land in just minutes or even seconds. Such floods are powerful, too. They can rip up trees and push boulders as though they were pebbles.

New Orleans

The city of New Orleans lies below sea level. Levees are used to keep the water out. When Hurricane Katrina struck in 2005, many levees failed. A huge area of land became flooded. About 2,000 people died in New Orleans and the greater area, while other people were stranded for days. The damages that came as a result of Katrina cost about $80 billion.

Mudslides are another type of flooding. They are caused by heavy rain on a bare, steep slope. Without rocks or plants to hold the land, a huge flow of watery mud may crash down on everything below it. Whole villages can be buried in seconds. Houses at the top of these slopes can crash down the hillside.

Floods may also come from the sea. Earthquakes may create giant waves called **tsunamis** (tsoo-NAH-mees). Tsunamis flood the shore. They may even stretch far inland. Such waves can flood buildings and pull loose items back into the ocean.

Floods can do great damage. They can destroy homes. They can ruin crops. People may drown or be stranded. Animals unable to reach higher land may be killed. Power may shut down. Bridges may be washed out. Supplies may be cut off from people who need them. Wastewater can back up from overflowing sewers. Then dirty water poisons the land. All living things may become ill long after the flood goes away.

A mudslide destroys a village in Honduras. It was caused by rains from Hurricane Mitch.

World's Worst Flood

Many floods happen along the Huang He (hwahng huah) River (also called the Yellow River) in China. The worst was in 1931. No one knows for sure how many people died, but the number is between 1 and 3.7 million. Between 1887 and 1943, more than 10 million people died as a result of floods along the river.

What Is a Blizzard?

Picture a heavy snowfall. Add extreme temperatures far below freezing. Mix in high winds and so much snow in the air that you can barely see. Stir everything together. Now you have a blizzard!

Blizzard winds travel at more than 56 kilometers (35 miles) per hour. Snow in the air makes it impossible to see more than 150 meters (492 feet) in the distance. In a severe blizzard, winds reach above 72 kilometers (45 miles) per hour. Temperatures drop to -12° C (10° F). Snow in the air makes it impossible to see at all.

In a blizzard, the snow in the air is not just snow falling from the sky. Winds are so strong that they lift snow from the ground. High winds also pile snow into tall drifts. Sometimes, these snowdrifts are higher than buildings!

a fierce blizzard in Finland

Antarctic Blizzard

It rarely snows heavily in the Antarctic. But the ground is always covered in snow. Strong winds whip the snow off the ground and drive it through the air. That makes an Antarctic blizzard.

Floods and Blizzards

What do they have in common? Both take a huge amount of water. The water is liquid in a flood. It is solid in a blizzard.

How the Blizzard Got Its Name

At one time, a blizzard meant heavy gunfire or a sharp blow. In 1870, an Iowa newspaper referred to a heavy snowstorm as a blizzard. The word caught on. Now it is the term everyone uses.

There can only be a blizzard if there is snow. Snow is made of ice crystals that precipitate from clouds. Snow forms from water vapor that rises high into the air. The vapor cools and condenses. It turns to water droplets. The droplets freeze if it is cold enough. They become ice crystals in clouds. The crystals connect to form snowflakes.

Snowflakes melt a little as they precipitate. They also collide with one another as they fall. Since they have melted a bit, they clump together easily. This is how they form little fluffs of snow.

The most common snowflakes have six sides. They look like lacy crystal stars.

Why does simple snowfall become a blizzard? Cold winds force vapor very quickly into the air. The air condenses. Huge amounts of snowflakes form. Then they precipitate. The flakes fall through very cold air. At the same time, warm air meets the cold air. Strong winds form where warm and cold air meet. Big snow and big winds make a blizzard.

There are always winds around Earth. The winds move mainly in the same direction. They move mainly west around the equator. They move mainly east around the poles. Westerly wind is warm and wet. Easterly wind is cold and icy. When the two winds meet, they have the right conditions for snow and even bigger winds.

Blizzards happen all over the world except near the equator. They happen most often in places where all the right conditions come together. This includes the far north and south of the world. It also includes very high places. The Great Plains and Great Lakes of North America often have blizzards. They are also common in northwest Europe. Russia, China, Korea, and Japan get them, too.

Winds that travel mainly east or west are called **prevailing winds**. That is because their normal direction prevails, or wins.

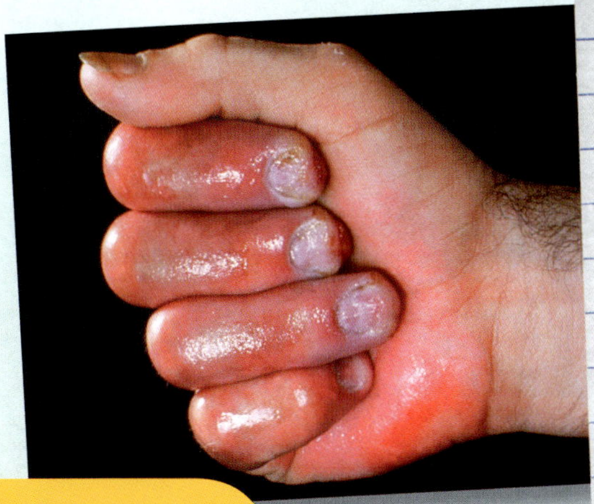

severe frostbite on a hand

Trouble for People

Blizzards can be dangerous to people. There are many accidents. People may freeze to death in the extreme cold. They may also develop **hypothermia** (hahy-puh-THUR-mee-uh) or **frostbite**. Frostbite is caused when tissue, or skin, becomes frozen. Hypothermia is caused by a big drop in body temperature.

What Floods and Blizzards Do to the Land

Floods and blizzards are awesome. They also have one important thing in common. They both depend on water.

It is said, "Water is a very good servant, but a cruel master." Water serves people well. But huge amounts of water on the loose can do great damage. It doesn't matter whether the water is in a liquid or solid form. Water's power is strong. Its path cannot be predicted.

On the other hand, water as a flood or blizzard is natural. It can do very good things for the land. Nature depends on floods and blizzards.

Words of Wisdom

Nothing on earth is so weak
and yielding as water,
Yet for breaking down that which is
firm and strong, it has no equal.
—Lao-Tzu, 6th century B.C.

A car sinks in a flood.

Water, whether liquid or solid, is at the heart of both floods and blizzards.

Floods can bring rich nutrients to an area such as this floodplain in Africa.

Floods cause problems for people. But that is because people may have built structures in the path of a flood. They may be caught in a flood themselves. But a flood is useful to nature.

Earth is always changing, and floods can help. For example, floods carry **sediments** from one place to another. Sediments are small bits of earth materials. The sediments have been **eroded** from rocks. This brings new soil to an area. It builds up new areas of land. And the soil brings nutrients with it. That means plants in the new area can get the nourishment they need. The soil stays **fertile**. It is ready for plants to grow.

What Is Erosion?

Erosion is the wearing away of land material by the action of water or wind.

Floods can also act as cleaners. They may flush out an area by carrying away dead matter. They mix up the matter and bury it somewhere else. This also helps to nourish the land. Plus, the large-scale movement of water can refill groundwater systems. A great deal of Earth's water is underground. It is important to life on Earth that the groundwater is present. It is even more important that it is clean and healthy.

There are some places in the world that depend on floods. Rice is an important crop in countries such as Indonesia and China. Rice crops need a lot of water. Floods help to bring the water to the rice. Terraced hillsides catch the floodwater so the rice can grow.

Farmers along the Nile River in Egypt have always counted on flooding. Floods bring new soil and water every year. They allow crops to grow in the floodplain. In ancient times, the flood god was an important one. People counted on the floods. Today, flooding is celebrated as a national holiday.

Weeping Goddess

The people of ancient Egypt believed that the flooding of the Nile was caused by sorrow. They said that Isis, a goddess, was crying over her dead husband, Osiris. Her tears created the flood.

Isis

Count on It

The ancient Egyptian calendar was based on the flood cycle. This shows how well the people could depend on the floods.

the Nile River floodplain

Terraces such as these help to trap floodwater for rice to grow.

Blizzards can have many of the same effects on land as floods have. The huge amount of snow and wind can erode the land. The snow also melts at some point. This creates massive amounts of water. The water may flood. If it does, it will behave in the same way that other floods behave. Sediments will be moved. Nutrients will be carried. Dead matter will be washed away and dropped someplace else.

An even more important thing about blizzards is that they provide more groundwater. Snow usually melts slowly. This gives the water time to seep into the ground. That allows more water to go into the ground for living things to use.

A glacier in New Zealand melts in a rush of water.

How Do They Compare?

It would take about 10 centimeters (4 inches) of snow, melted, to equal 1 centimeter (.4 inches) of water.

A blizzard brings its own troubles. But when the snow melts, the trouble may be even greater.

These people are building a barrier to try to prevent flooding.

Be Prepared!

The first thing for a person to do is to pay attention. Watch the weather and listen to weather reports. Weather scientists have learned a lot about predicting floods and blizzards. Check the Internet. Listen to the news on the TV or radio. There will be updates and warnings there.

People should also keep emergency supplies. These include canned food, water, flashlights, batteries, first aid supplies, and blankets. Everything should be kept in a waterproof bin.

It may also be a good idea to talk with emergency workers. Ask them what to do in case of a flood or blizzard. They will help you know how to protect yourself and your loved ones. Chances are, you will not be caught in a flood or blizzard. But if you are, you will be glad that you were prepared!

Keeping supplies such as candles, flashlights, and clean water in one place will help you prepare for an emergency.

Lab: Eroding Earth

Erosion can result after fires or floods have swept through an area. This lab activity will help you to see what happens.

Materials

- dry, loose soil
- cheesecloth
- spray bottle and water, or hose with misting sprayer and a water source
- digital camera (optional)

Procedure:

1. Using dry loose soil, build a small steep hill about .6 meters (2 feet) across.
2. If a digital camera is available, take a photo of the hill to help with your observation.
3. Completely cover the hill with cheesecloth.
4. Take another photo of the hill, if a camera is available.

5. Using a spray bottle or a misting sprayer attached to a hose, apply water to the cloth-covered hill for a short time and watch what happens. Take photos during the spraying and after. Does the hill lose its shape? What happens to the soil? Does everything just stay in place but only get wet?

6. Remove the cheesecloth. (This is similar to what happens when vegetation is removed from a hill or mountainside.) Take another photo.

7. Using the spray bottle or misting sprayer attached to a hose, apply water to the hill again for a short time and watch what happens. Take photos during and after. What happens to the soil? What happens to the hill? Does everything stay in place?

8. What can you conclude, based on your experiment?

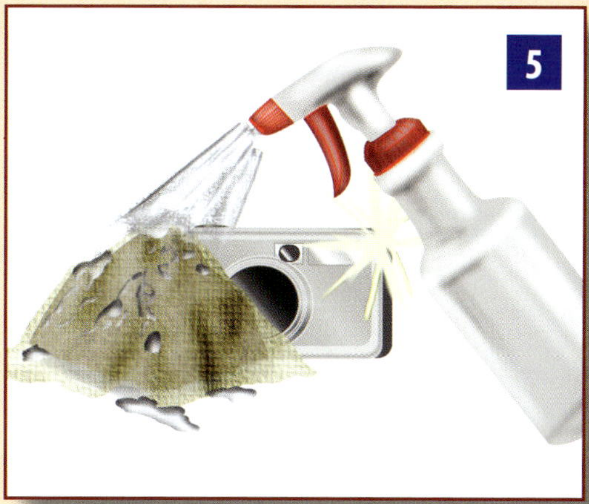

Glossary

blizzard—a storm with high winds, heavy snow, and intense cold

condense—when a gas turns into a liquid

cumulonimbus—a thunderstorm cloud with large, dense towers that reach high into the atmosphere

erode—wear away through water or wind

evaporate—when a liquid turns into a gas or vapor

fertile—able to produce life such as plants

flash flood—a sudden and powerful rush of water down a slope or gully

flood—a large overflow of water onto an area that is not usually submersed

floodplain—low, flat land alongside a river or stream that is often flooded

frostbite—a condition caused when a person's body tissue becomes frozen, resulting in numbing, swelling, and discoloration and possibly requiring the affected area to be removed

hypothermia—a condition caused by a drop in a person's body temperature, resulting in shivering, drowsiness, disorientation, and death if not treated

mudslide—a massive, sudden rush of watery mud down a slope, usually resulting from a heavy rain on a hillside empty of plant life

precipitate—to fall to Earth as water in the form of rain, snow, or hail

prevailing winds—winds that travel in a regular direction (west near the equator and east near the poles)

sediments—minerals or living matter deposited by water or air

tsunami—a giant wave caused by an undersea earthquake, volcanic eruption, undersea landslide, or meteor strike

Index

Scientists Then and Now

Wladimir Köppen
(1846–1940)

Wladimir Köppen grew up in Russia. He studied botany, climate, and weather. As an adult, he traveled a lot. He saw that the places he visited had very different types of plants. These differences made him curious. So, he studied the differences and found that temperature had big effects on plants. He developed the Köppen climate classification system. This system is still used by scientists.

Jagdish Shukla
(1944–)

Jagdish Shukla was born in a small village in India. He wanted to study science in school, but his school did not teach it. His father got science books for him, and Shukla taught himself. Today, he is a science professor and does research on weather and climate. He has helped people to better understand the weather and climates of the world. He has received many important awards for his work.

Image Credits

Cover Jocelyn Augustino/FEMA; p.1 Jocelyn Augustino/FEMA; p.4 Digital Wisdom/LKPalmer; p.4-5 Howard Grill/Shutterstock; p.5(top) Marc van Vuren/Shutterstock; p.5(bottom) ©2009 Jupiterimages Corporation; p.6 TobagoCays/Shutterstock; p.7(top) Tim Bradley; p.7(bottom) Andrew Chin/Shutterstock; p.8 Deshakalyan Chowdhury/AFP/Getty Images; p.8(bottom) Jocelyn Augustino/FEMA; p.10-11 Yuri Cortez/AFP/Getty Images; p.12-13 Dainis Derics/Shutterstock; p.13 blickwinkel/Alamy; p.14 ©David Arky/Corbis; p.14-15 Stephanie Reid; p.15(bottom) Newscom; p.16 Stephanie Reid; p.17(top) Southern Illinois University/Photo Researchers, Inc.; p16-17 Shutterstock; p.18-19 Johnandersonphoto/Dreamstime; p.19(top) Four Oaks/Shutterstock; p.19(bottom left) Tischenko Irina/Shutterstock; p.19(bottom right) ELEN/Shutterstock; p.20-21 Anthony Bannister/Photo Researchers, Inc.; p.21 Brenda Tharp/Photo Researchers, Inc.; p.22 Vladimir Wrangel/Shutterstock; p.22-23 Ng Wei Keong/Shutterstock; p.23 Louise Cukrov/Shutterstock; p.24 Johnathan Esper/Shutterstock; p.24-25 Daniel Gratton/Shutterstock; p.26 Steve Skjold/Alamy; p.26-27 Joe Rivera/Shutterstock; p.26-27(front) Nic Neish/Shutterstock; p.28-29 Tim Bradley; p.32(left) Rick Reason; p.32(right) Evan Cantwell, George Mason University.